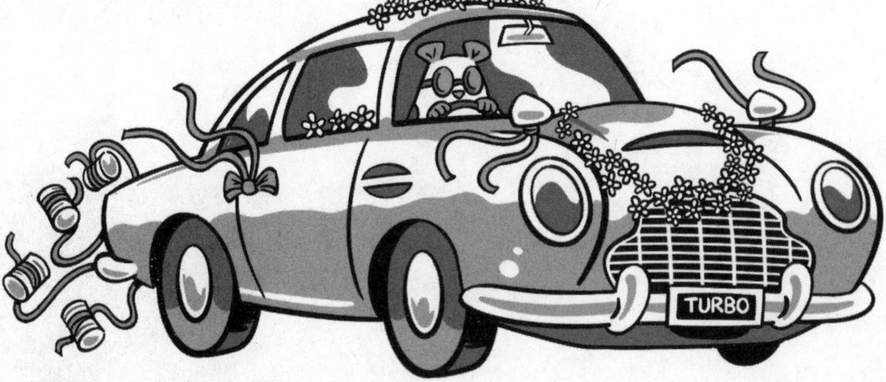
TURBO

CAPTAIN AWESOME

IS A SPY!

By STAN KIRBY

Illustrated by DOC MORAN

LITTLE SIMON

New York   London   Toronto   Sydney   New Delhi

LITTLE SIMON

An imprint of Simon & Schuster Children's Publishing Division • 1230 Avenue of the Americas, New York, New York 10020 • First Little Simon hardcover edition July 2023 • Copyright © 2023 by Simon & Schuster, Inc. • Also available in a Little Simon paperback edition. • All rights reserved, including the right of reproduction in whole or in part in any form. • LITTLE SIMON is a registered trademark of Simon & Schuster, Inc., and associated colophon is a trademark of Simon & Schuster, Inc. • For information about special discounts for bulk purchases, please contact Simon & Schuster Special Sales at 1-866-506-1949 or business@simonandschuster.com. • The Simon & Schuster Speakers Bureau can bring authors to your live event. • For more information or to book an event, contact the Simon & Schuster Speakers Bureau at 1-866-248-3049 or visit our website at www.simonspeakers.com. • Designed by Chani Yammer. • The text of this book was set in Little Simon Gazette.

Manufactured in the United States of America 0623 LAK

10 9 8 7 6 5 4 3 2 1

This book has been cataloged with the Library of Congress.

ISBN 978-1-6659-3283-7 (hc)

ISBN 978-1-6659-3282-0 (pbk)

ISBN 978-1-6659-3284-4 (ebook)

Table of Contents

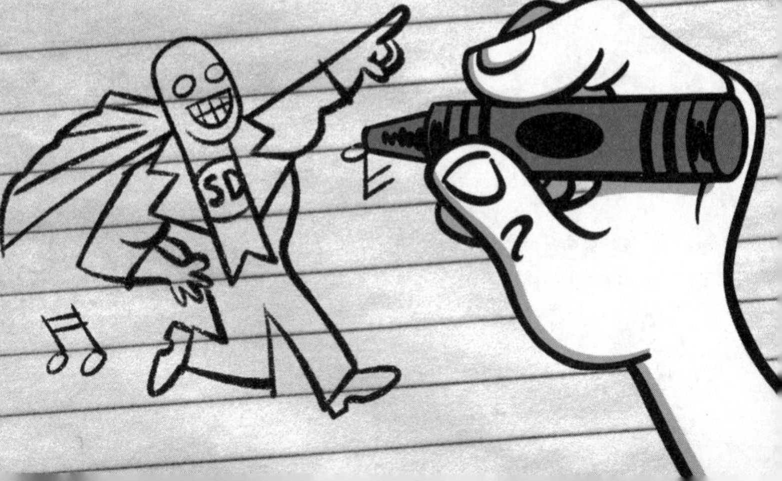

SD

CHAPTER 1

Waffle Fever!

By
Eugene

SNIFF! SMELL! SMILE!

Eugene's Awesome-Sense was tingling. But he wasn't smelling danger. He wasn't even sensing it. This was not a job for **Captain Awesome**.

It was waffles! Melted butter! The power of maple syrup!

"This is a job for *me*!" Eugene yelled. "Here comes the one and only **Breakfast Devourer**!"

Eugene threw back his Super

Dude blanket and leaped from his bed. He changed out of his Super Dude pajamas and slipped into his Super Dude sneakers. He shot out of his bedroom like a missile from Missile Master's missile blaster in Super Dude No. 229.

Who is Super Dude, you ask? Super Dude is the greatest superhero ever! He's the star of Super Dude comic books, TV shows, movies, and supercool clothes, too. Most importantly, he's Eugene's inspiration. With his best friends, Sally and Charlie, they formed the epic **Sunnyview Superhero Squad**.

"Hi, Mom!" Eugene said as he slid into his seat at the kitchen table. "Waffle me!"

"Waffles up!" Eugene's mom beamed. She set down a plate on the table with two round waffles.

Eugene took in a big whiff of waffle air. He stuffed a double-size bite into his mouth. "They taste even better than they smell."

Eugene's mom set down a plate of bacon. "And just for you, my little angel," she said. "Your favorite!"

"BACON!" Eugene cheered.

That's when Eugene's Awesome-Sense went off again, even stronger than before. **Little angel? Waffles . . . *and* bacon?**

His mom was up to something.

"Am I supposed to go to the dentist today?" he asked, suspicious.

"Why no, dear. Not the dentist." She paused. It was the kind of pause a

mom makes when she's getting ready to tell you something terrible. Was broccoli on sale? Were they having cucumber-and-liver sandwiches for dinner?

"However, we've been invited to the Perriwinkles' wedding! Isn't that exciting?" Eugene's mom asked.

"Wait. What? A wedding?!"
Eugene exclaimed. "And who are
the Perristinkles?"

"The Perri*winkles*," his mom corrected him. "They're old family friends, and one of them is getting married!"

Eugene frowned. "Ugh, weddings are gross! They're so lovey-dovey."

"There's also a dance floor," Eugene's mom pointed out.

Eugene was still frowning.

"But I forgot the best part," his mom continued. "There will be a huge cake with lots of icing!"

"You mean I have to go too?!" Not even the delicious waffles could save Eugene now.

His mom waved a fancy envelope with ribbons and lace in front of his face. "The invitation arrived a bit late, so we'll have to get you a new suit right away. The wedding is this weekend."

Eugene froze. "The. Wedding. Is. This. Weekend?"

"Won't that be fun?" His mom smiled.

"That's the *opposite* of fun, Mom," Eugene said. "Charlie and Sally and I were going to have a Super Dude reading party this weekend!"

"A what?"

"Super Dude's new Ultra-Mega Edition came out this week. There's stickers, a poster, and a Super Dude mini-figure. A *mini-figure*, Mom!"

Eugene's mom grabbed her purse. "Well, your Super Dude reading party will have to wait until the Perriwinkles' ultra-mega wedding is over. Now, let's get you a suit!"

Eugene sighed. He took the last bite of his waffle. As he left, he grabbed the extra waffle sitting on the kitchen counter and stuffed it in his backpack. If he was trying on a suit (*ugh!*) for a wedding (*ugh!*), he was going to need lots of waffle energy.

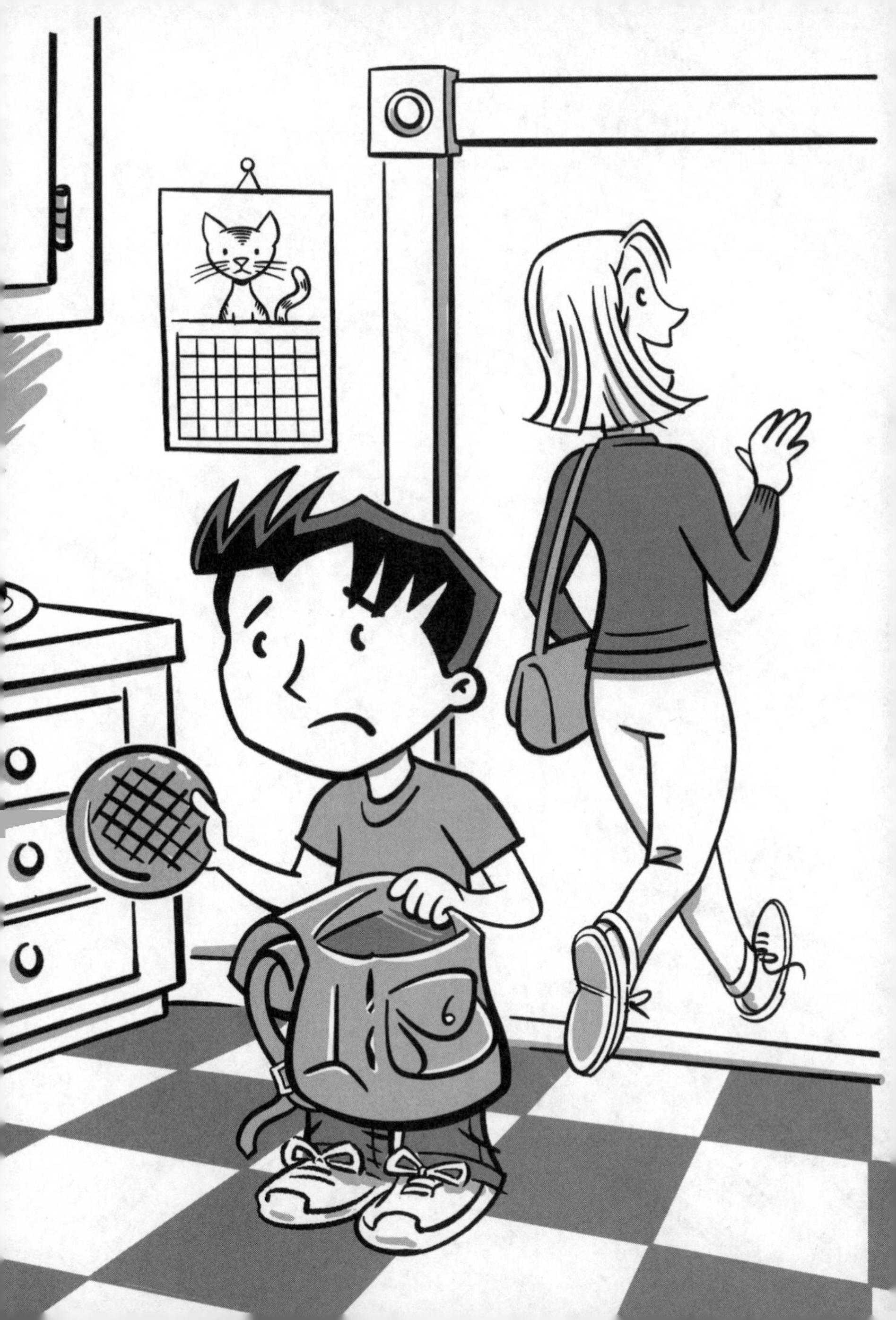

CHAPTER 2

The Tuxedo of Awesomeness

By
Eugene

"ACK!
"GRUFFLE!
"SNARF!"

"How does that fit you, young Mr. McGillicudy?" Mr. Soot asked Eugene.

Eugene and his mother had been at Mr. Soot's Go-Go Suit Shop for nearly thirty minutes. Eugene was trying on his fourth suit.

"The tie is pulling on my neck like Twisto the Evil Clown, the

jacket is squeezing my body like Colonel Juice Squeezer, and the pants are sticking to my legs like Mr. S. Tic Cling!" Eugene cried. "I'm being attacked from all sides!"

"I think that you look very handsome," Eugene's mom said.

Moms are always saying goopy stuff like that, Eugene thought. *It's their job.*

"Take a look in the mirror," Mr. Soot said. "See what others will see."

Eugene stopped struggling. The evil clothes had won—for now.

As Eugene began to turn around, that's when he saw it. Awesomeness in the shape of a jacket and bow tie! Over there!

"Whoa . . . what kind of suit is that?!" Eugene pointed to a tuxedo on a hanger. It was shiny and slick, and it made all the other suits look not so cool.

"That's a tuxedo," Mr. Soot said.

"And by tuxedo, you mean . . . **a spy suit**," Eugene replied. "If I have to go to a wedding, I want to look like that!"

Eugene put on the tuxedo in a flash and leaped out from the changing room. He adjusted his collar and straightened his jacket.

Just like a spy! Eugene thought, looking at his reflection. "Whoa! Looking super cool!" a voice said.

The store's bell rang as Charlie Thomas Jones and his mom walked in. Charlie was Eugene's best friend. He was also Nacho Cheese Man from the Sunnyview Superhero Squad.

"I want a spy suit like Eugene, please!" Charlie said to his mom. He turned to Mr. Soot. Charlie held up a can of jalapeño spray cheese. "With pockets for my cheese."

"Why do you need a tuxedo?" Eugene asked.

"We're going to a meeting of the Legion of Perriwinkles," Charlie said.

"The Legion of Perriwinkles sounds awesome!" It took Eugene a moment to register that. "Wait a second . . . you're going to the wedding too?"

"Yeah. I guess this means we aren't having our Super Dude reading party this weekend, huh?" Charlie didn't look thrilled about this.

"Nope. Talk about an evil way to spend a weekend." Eugene sighed.

Charlie squirted a blast of jalapeño cheese into his mouth. "Nothing more evil than a wedding," he agreed.

CHAPTER 3

I Spy

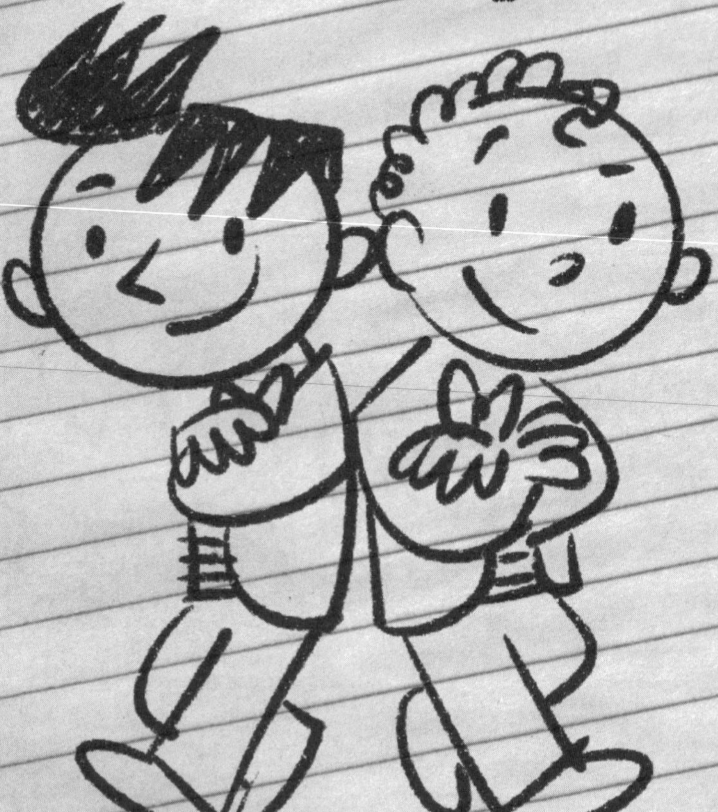

By
Eugene

"I'm already bored." Eugene, his parents, and Charlie stood in the doorway of the church. Eugene adjusted his collar. "My shirt has my neck in the grip of doom!"

"We look like the Sunnyview Tuxedo Squad!" Charlie joked.

Eugene put on a pair of dark sunglasses. "Mom, take a photo!"

CLICK!

Eugene's mom snapped a couple of pictures with her phone as Eugene and Charlie did spy poses. "Your dad and I are going to find our seats. Meet us at our bench," she said.

Charlie turned to Eugene. "Why are all the decorations white or pink?"

"Dunno, but I really hope Little Miss Stinky Pinky isn't here." Eugene shivered. "This totally seems like a place she'd be during the weekend."

Little Miss Stinky Pinky (aka Meredith Mooney) was Eugene's mean classmate. If she was here, it would make things even stinkier and pinker.

Charlie picked up a balloon filled with glitter. "No more pink talk! Glitter ball!"

He swatted the balloon to Eugene.

"Captain Awesome powers, unleash!" Eugene laughed and swatted it back. But when Charlie hit the balloon again, it sailed just out of Eugene's reach and headed toward a hallway.

Eugene chased
the balloon down
the hall. He jumped
on a chair, flew into
the air . . . and caught it! He dropped
to the floor in front of a closed door.

A sweet scent came out from under the door. It made Eugene's belly rumble.

I'll bet the huge cake's in there, he thought. *Maybe I could just take a peek. . . .*

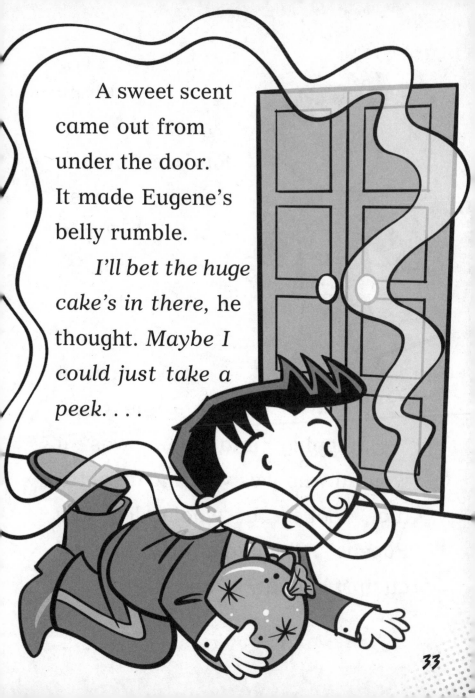

Eugene reached for the doorknob, but the door flew open before he could even turn it. He jumped back, pressing himself flat against the wall.

Stepping into view was a woman who was wearing an outfit that looked a whole lot like Eugene's. She had a finger pressed against her ear.

". . . Immediately," she was whispering. "It's an emergency. . . . Keep it secret. . . . Take it before anyone else sees. . . . Don't tell them. . . ."

With those mysterious words, she ran down the hall.

Eugene gasped. This wasn't normal boring wedding stuff. **This was secret agent spy stuff!**

He started to follow the woman,
who was so clearly a spy. But just
then wedding music started to play.

Oh no! The spy's going to get away! Eugene thought. He wanted to follow her . . . but maybe it would be best with backup.

Eugene dropped the balloon and raced to his seat with Charlie.

CHAPTER 4

The Mushy Stuff Is Here

By
Eugene

The flower girls were dressed in pink and white. They carried violet carnations in their hands as they walked down the center aisle on the pink carpet.

Eugene whispered to Charlie, "Keep your eyes open for anything odd."

"What's odd is that the flower girls aren't carrying pink or white flowers," Charlie said. "It doesn't go with the theme!"

"Not that!" Eugene whispered. "I saw something in the hallway that was very suspicious."

"Was it her?" Charlie asked.

Eugene turned as everyone in the church stood to face the back door. The bride stepped into the

doorway wearing a pink-and-white dress. A white veil covered her face.

"Oooh," the guests said dreamily.

But Eugene didn't have time to ooh and aah over a big fluffy dress! There was work to do.

"In the hallway, there was a spy!" he told Charlie. "She was being very suspicious, like running around! Do you see anything strange?"

Charlie inspected the room, then shook his head. "Nope," he replied. "Just people dressed up."

"But—" Eugene started to say, but the lady in front of them turned to glare.

"Young sirs!" she whispered angrily. "Shh!"

Eugene huffed. Maybe she was in league with the spies!

As soon as the lady turned around, Eugene was back to plotting. "My mom said that the reception is in the room next door. Once all of this mushy stuff is over, we'll get to the bottom of this."

"We *are* dressed like superspies," Charlie noted. "Wait, we're not going to miss the cake part, are we? I'm only here for the cake."

"Of course not," Eugene promised him.

The bride reached the altar, where her groom happily waited, and everyone sat down.

"Dearly beloved," the priest began. "We are gathered here today to celebrate the eternal love between these two people, Doug Chaykin and Amanda Perriwinkle."

BLAH. BLAH. BLAH.

As Doug and Amanda said their vows, Eugene noticed something he hadn't seen before. There was another door in the room, one behind the altar. The door had a small window, and someone was looking into the wedding.

"Charlie! Charlie, look!" Eugene hissed, pointing at the door.

The boys craned their necks to inspect what was happening. Just like the last time Eugene had seen her, the spy brought her finger to her ear, whispered something, and rushed off.

"Holy mozzarella!" Charlie said. "You're right! There IS a spy at the Perriwinkles' wedding!"

The lady in front of them turned around again. "Shh!"

But that didn't matter. After the wedding ceremony, Eugene and Charlie would go spy on a spy.

CHAPTER 5

The Cheese Arrives

By Eugene

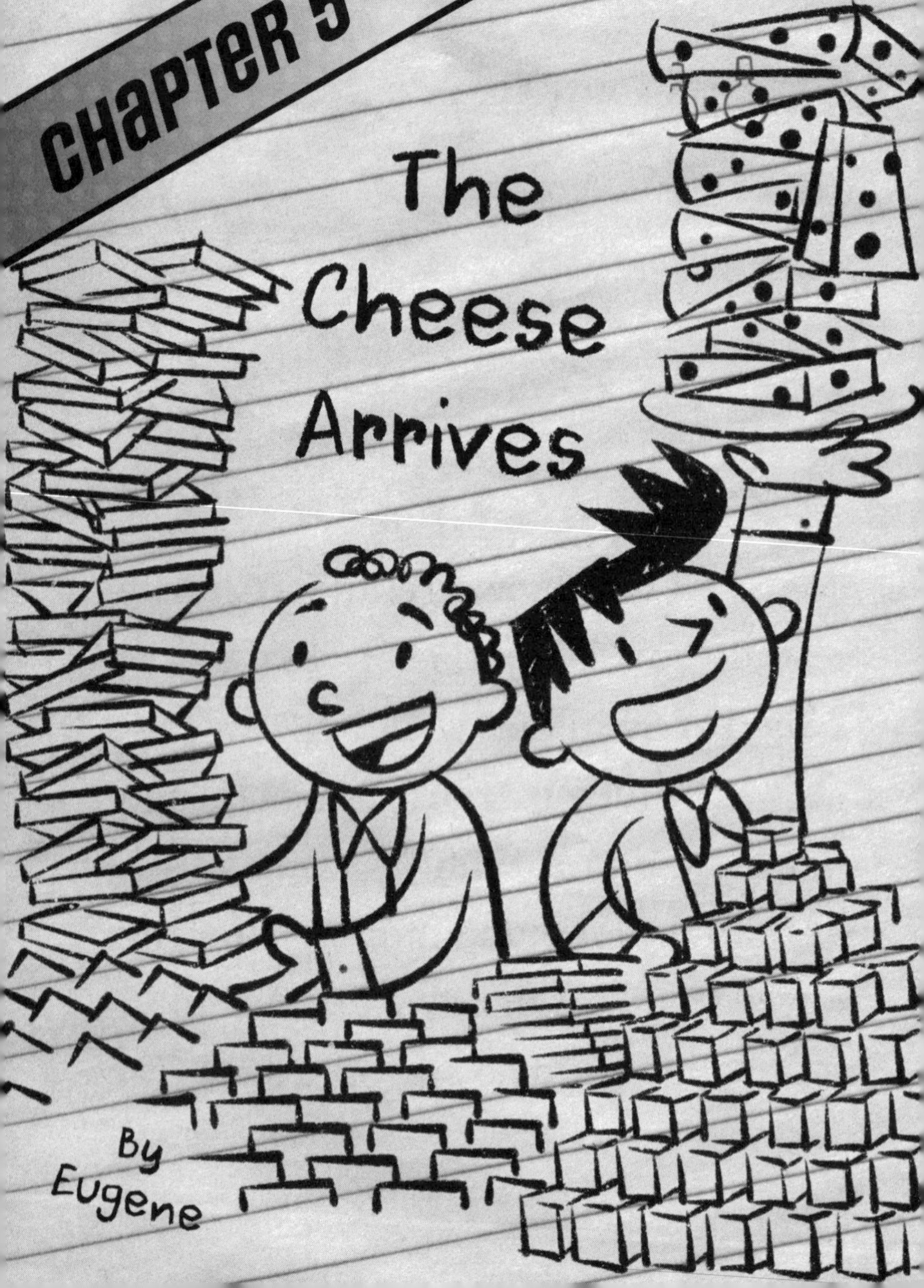

"Wow!" Charlie exclaimed. "I've never seen so many lights in one room."

Once the bride and groom ended the ceremony with a kiss (*ugh!*), everyone moved over to the reception room. The DJ played music underneath a colorful disco ball, and the guests were dancing the night away.

Well, everyone except Eugene and Charlie. They stood by the reception doors.

"Eyes open," Eugene ordered. "Everyone is a suspect!"

Charlie was dancing in place. "How long are we going to stand here for? I hate to say it, but this DJ is amazing!"

"Long enough to find out where the spy is . . . aha! There!" Eugene pointed at a sliver of black and white moving through the guests.

"Let's follow her before we lose her again," Charlie suggested.

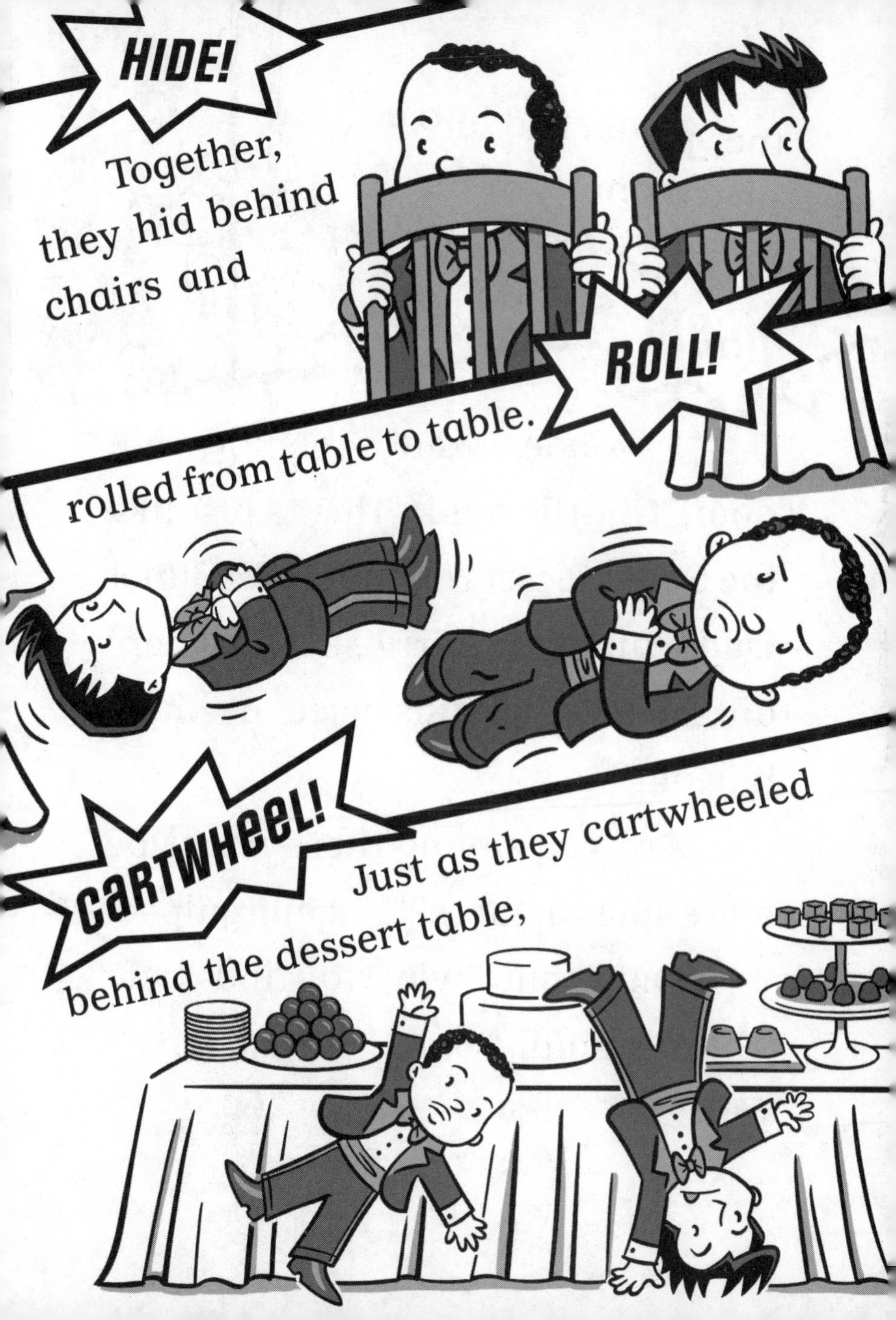
HIDE!
Together, they hid behind chairs and
ROLL!
rolled from table to table.
CARTWHEEL!
Just as they cartwheeled behind the dessert table,

the spy ducked into a new room.

DUCK!

"I wonder what's behind that door," Charlie said. "This is just like the Supersecret Hideout from Super Dude number thirty-seven, where all the evil villains used a single hideout!"

"Are you saying there might be more spies in there?" Eugene gulped.

"Only one way to find out," Charlie said. "One . . . two . . . THREE!"

They burst into the room with cool poses ready. But . . . there was no one there.

"It's just a kitchen!" Eugene said. "Definitely not the Supersecret Hideout."

Charlie sniffed the air. "My Nacho Cheese Man powers are telling me there's cheese nearby. Brie . . . maybe Camembert, too!"

"Let's look for any hidden cameras or spy drones," Eugene said.

"Found it!" Charlie exclaimed.

Eugene asked, "Hidden cameras? Maybe spy drones?"

"Nope," Charlie said. "This incredible plate of cheese triangles and crackers of different shapes!"

Eugene looked at the table covered with plates of cheese. He couldn't resist them.

"Okay, snack time, then spy time," Eugene said. He grabbed two cheese triangles.

"Dude," Charlie said as he ate. "I've never seen so many kinds of cheese in one place before! There's **mozzarella, feta, cheddar, Gouda, and Gorgonzola,** all sliced perfectly!"

Eugene ate another cheese and chewed slowly. The flavors were so delicious, so good. . . .

"Wait! It's a trap." Eugene shoved the cheeses away.

Charlie frowned. "From the spies?"

"Yes!" Eugene hissed. "They want us to be distracted by the delicious cheeses so we won't realize what they're up to!"

"I'm a bit lost," Charlie admitted.

"They want to . . . uh . . ." Eugene paused. What did he actually know about these very suspicious spy-waiters?

He shook his head. "We'll have to find out. But look!"

Two of the waitstaff entered the kitchen. Charlie and Eugene ducked behind a shiny metal cart that was covered in a pink-and-white cloth.

"It's her, with another spy," Eugene whispered.

"We're on our way!" the spy-waitress said, pressing a finger to her ear.

"We have to do this, before it's too late!" the waiter added.

They picked up trays of salami and dashed out.

"Okay, that *is* pretty weird," Charlie said. He grabbed another cheese triangle. "If only we had the complete Sunnyview Superhero Squad here."

CHAPTER 6

Spying on the Spies!

By Eugene

"Psst! Over here!" Eugene and Charlie suddenly heard a voice whisper as they snuck back out the kitchen doors.

"Who said that?" Charlie asked.

"It must be the spymaster!" Eugene gasped. "Show yourself!"

"It's me!" the voice said. "Down here!"

Psst!

As Eugene looked down, he saw Sally Williams, the third and final member of the Sunnyview Superhero Squad, peeking out from under the tablecloth of the wedding present table.

"Come on!" she whispered.

Eugene and Charlie dove under the table, and Sally quickly lowered the tablecloth so no one would see them.

"Sally?! By all that's super, am I glad to see you!" Eugene exclaimed. Then a realization hit him. "Wait. Why are you here?"

"Me?! What are *you two* doing at my cousin's wedding?!" Sally asked.

"Your cousin is a Perriwinkle?" Eugene said.

"Cool hiding place," Charlie added.

"I'm not hiding," Sally explained. "I'm *spying* . . . on the spies!"

"You saw them too?" Eugene asked.

"Yeah! I've been watching them talk on the spy walkie-talkies in their ears," Sally replied. "I don't know what their plan is yet, but maybe we can figure it out as a team."

"That's a great idea! Sunnyview Superhero Squad . . . ASSEMBLE!" Eugene called out.

"We've never assembled under a table before. It's kinda cool," Charlie said.

Sally reached into her jacket and pulled out a notebook. "I've been keeping track of everything the spies have been doing."

"**MI-TEE!**" Eugene exclaimed. "Show us what you've got."

Sally handed her notes to Eugene.

"They've been disappearing to do secret missions," Sally explained. "And they're always talking to someone on their spy headsets."

"Do you think they're trying to mess something up?" Charlie asked.

"They're trying to do more than mess *something* up, Charlie. They're trying to mess EVERYTHING up," Eugene said. "Spies call it . . . *sabotage!*"

"Who'd want to sabotage my cousin's wedding?" Sally asked.

"I bet it's the dessert-y do-badder, the Tiramisunami! She wants to wipe out the wedding with waves of bitter chocolate!"

"I bet they're going to steal the wedding rings!" Sally said.

"And all the wedding presents!" Charlie guessed.

"That would only ruin the wedding for the bride and groom," Eugene said. "I think they're going to steal something so important, it would ruin it for everyone ... even us!"

Eugene lifted the tablecloth and pointed.

"That!" Eugene said.

SHOCK!

GASP!

DOUBLE GASP!

"They're going to cake-nap the wedding cake!" Eugene cried.

CHAPTER 7

Over and Out . . . of Cake!

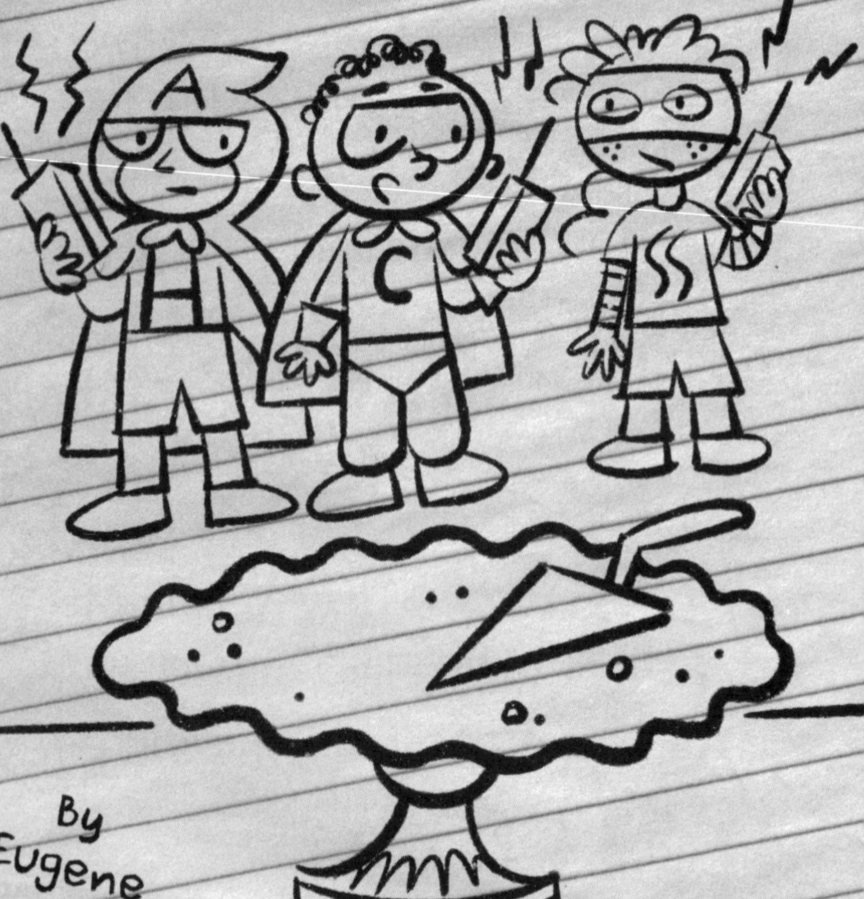

By Eugene

"We can't let them steal the wedding cake! I've got a can of cheese-flavored frosting to spray on my slice!" Charlie whipped out his can of cheese frosting and sprayed some into his mouth. "So good."

"My super senses are telling me it's worse than that," Eugene began. "I bet they're going to steal the cake and replace it with something evil like . . . pecan pie!"

Eugene shook his head in disappointment.

"P-p-p-pecan pie?!" Charlie stammered in horror. "What kind of evil mad person makes a pie out of *nuts*?!"

"The same kind that puts raisins in cookies," Eugene answered. "We have to stop these evil spies! Not just for the bride and groom! Not just for the guests! But for every kid who's ever had to sit through a wedding with the hope of getting cake as their only reward!"

BACKPACKS!
CAPES!
SUPERHERO TIME!

Eugene, Charlie, and Sally may have crawled under the table, but it was Captain Awesome, Nacho Cheese Man, and Supersonic Sal who crawled out!

Supersonic Sal retrieved three Super Dude walkie-talkies from her backpack and passed them to the boys.

"Super Dude Supersonic Walkies, activated!" she announced.

"Whoa!" Captain Awesome said. "Where'd you get these?"

"My parents gave them to me as a gift on my last birthday. I've been saving them for the perfect time," Supersonic Sal explained.

"Nacho Cheese Man, reporting for superhero duty. Over," Nacho Cheese Man said into his walkie-talkie. "You're supposed to say 'over' at the end so everyone knows you're done talking. Over."

"Why don't we split up?" Captain Awesome suggested. "Use your walkie-talkies if you see anything evil going on!"

"Besides an evil vegetable platter?" Nacho Cheese Man asked.

"Yes, besides that," Captain Awesome replied.

With walkie-talkies in their hands and courage in their hearts, the three heroes were about to split up when they realized . . . **THE CAKE WAS ALREADY GONE!**

"No!" Supersonic Sal said. "That really takes the cake!"

"We didn't even get a chance to use the walkie-talkies. Over,"Nacho Cheese Man sadly said into his walkie.

"Use your hypersonic cake-finding powers!" Captain Awesome cried. "We've got to find the cake before this wedding becomes a full-on cake-tastrophe!"

"I've spotted the cake! I repeat! I've spotted the cake! Over," Nacho Cheese Man said into his walkie-talkie.

"Uh, Nacho Cheese Man, we're standing right next to you," Supersonic Sal pointed out. "We can hear you *without* the walkie-talkie."

"I know," Nacho Cheese Man replied. "But I just really, really want to use it."

Captain Awesome saw the two spies rolling the cake into the next room on a cart.

"Hold your capes!" Captain Awesome said. "They're cutting through the dance floor!"

"It's time to dance our way to defeating evil," Nacho Cheese Man said, then raised the walkie-talkie to his mouth. "Over and out!"

CHAPTER 8

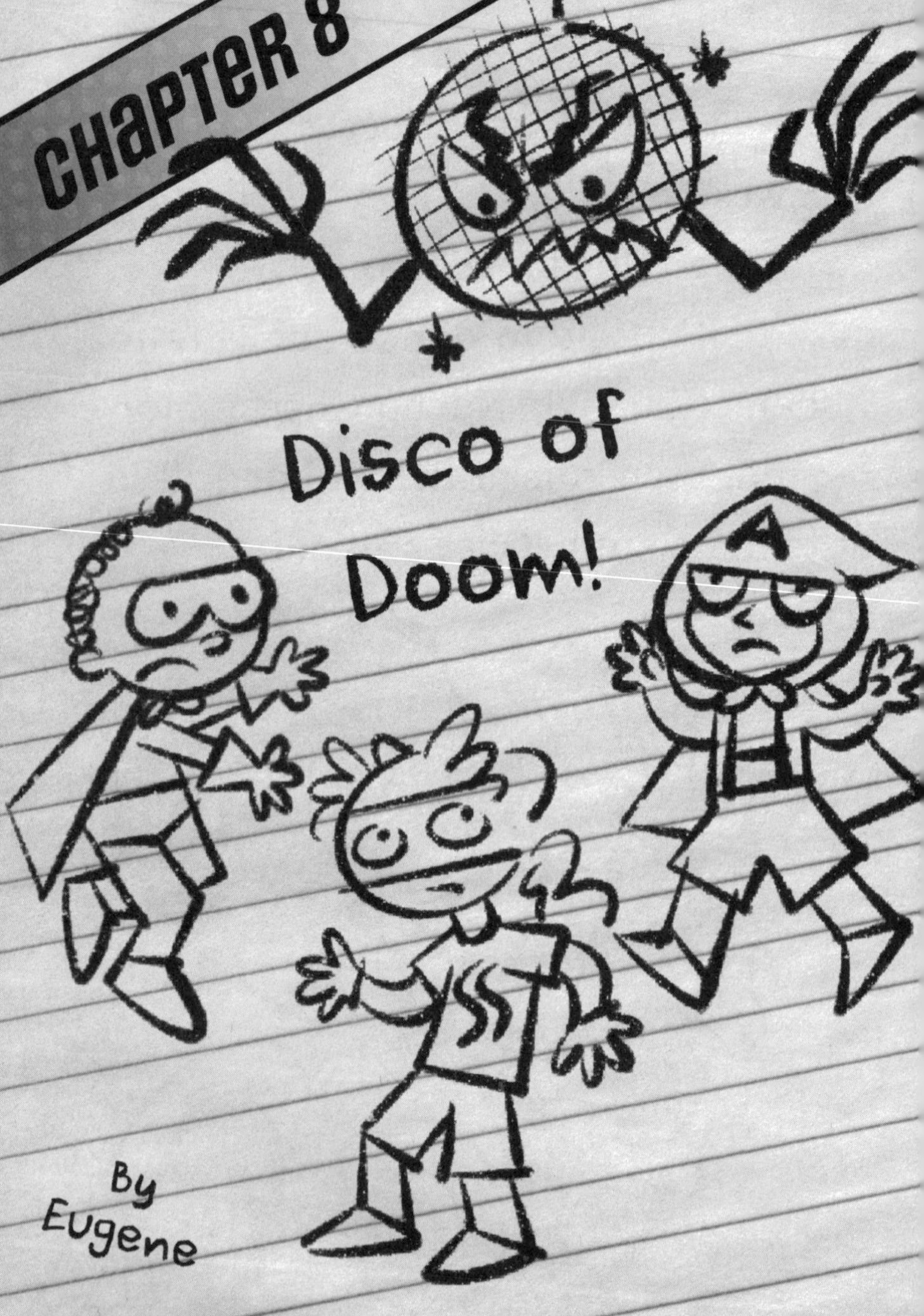
Disco of Doom!
By Eugene

Captain Awesome, Supersonic Sal, and Nacho Cheese Man ran into the room. Disco music filled the air, and colored lights flashed overhead.

"Whoa . . . ," Captain Awesome said. "Now that we're actually on the dance floor, this isn't as evil as I thought."

"The dance floor isn't, but the waiters sure are," Nacho Cheese Man said. "There's the cake!"

The spy-waiters rushed toward a door on the opposite side of the dance floor with the cake.

"They're going to *cake*scape!" Supersonic Sal cried out. "That door leads outside!"

"Dance charge, now!" Captain Awesome cried.

The heroes started to run-dance their way across the dance floor, but Captain Awesome was suddenly swept up by a conga line!

"Help!" Captain Awesome called out as he conga'd away. "I'm stuck in the rhythm of 'doom, doom, doom-doom'!"

Nacho Cheese Man leaped to the side and avoided the conga line, but he landed in the middle of dancers doing the "Cha-Cha Slide."

"Slide to the left! Slide to the right! Reverse! Reverse! Cha-cha now, y'all!" the DJ sang.

"The power of cha-cha . . . is too strong!" Nacho Cheese Man gasped. "Got . . . to . . . slide to the right . . . slide to the left . . ."

"It's up to you, Supersonic Sal!" Captain Awesome shouted as the conga line danced past. "Can't . . . stop . . . dancing!"

Supersonic Sal covered her ears. She raced across the dance floor, spinning past wedding guests doing the "Macarena," but found herself in the middle of a group practicing "Y.M.C.A." Supersonic Sal instantly thrust her arms above her head to make the letter Y!

"The spies must be using . . .
mind-control music!" Supersonic
Sal's arms curled over her head to
make the letter *M*. "But I'll never be
stopped . . . by a disco song!"

The fate of the wedding cake was in her hands! Supersonic Sal mustered all her supersonic powers and fought the urge to make a large C with the other dancers.

Supersonic Sal broke the musical mind control. She raced to the DJ table and unplugged the speakers. The music stopped.

"Awwwww!" the wedding guests groaned in unison.

Captain Awesome and Nacho Cheese Man breathed shakily.

"Are you two okay?" Supersonic Sal asked.

"Yeah, but it reminds me of the time Super Dude fought the Disco Dreadfuls to save Funky Town in Super Dude number one hundred nineteen," Captain Awesome replied. "The Bumble Bee Gees flew in at the last second to save the day, just like you did!"

"I think we stopped the mind control for good," Supersonic Sal said. "Turn the music back on, and let's find those spies!"

Nacho Cheese Man gave himself a dose of canned cheese to regain his strength. Then he plugged the speakers back in. To the delight of everyone around, the music started up again.

With the wedding guests happily dancing to music that *wouldn't* melt their brains, the trio of heroes ran out the door to follow the two spies.

Once outside, the superheroes saw something more shocking than Nacho Cheese Man's dancing skills. It was the spies loading the cake into a van. They were going to make their escape!

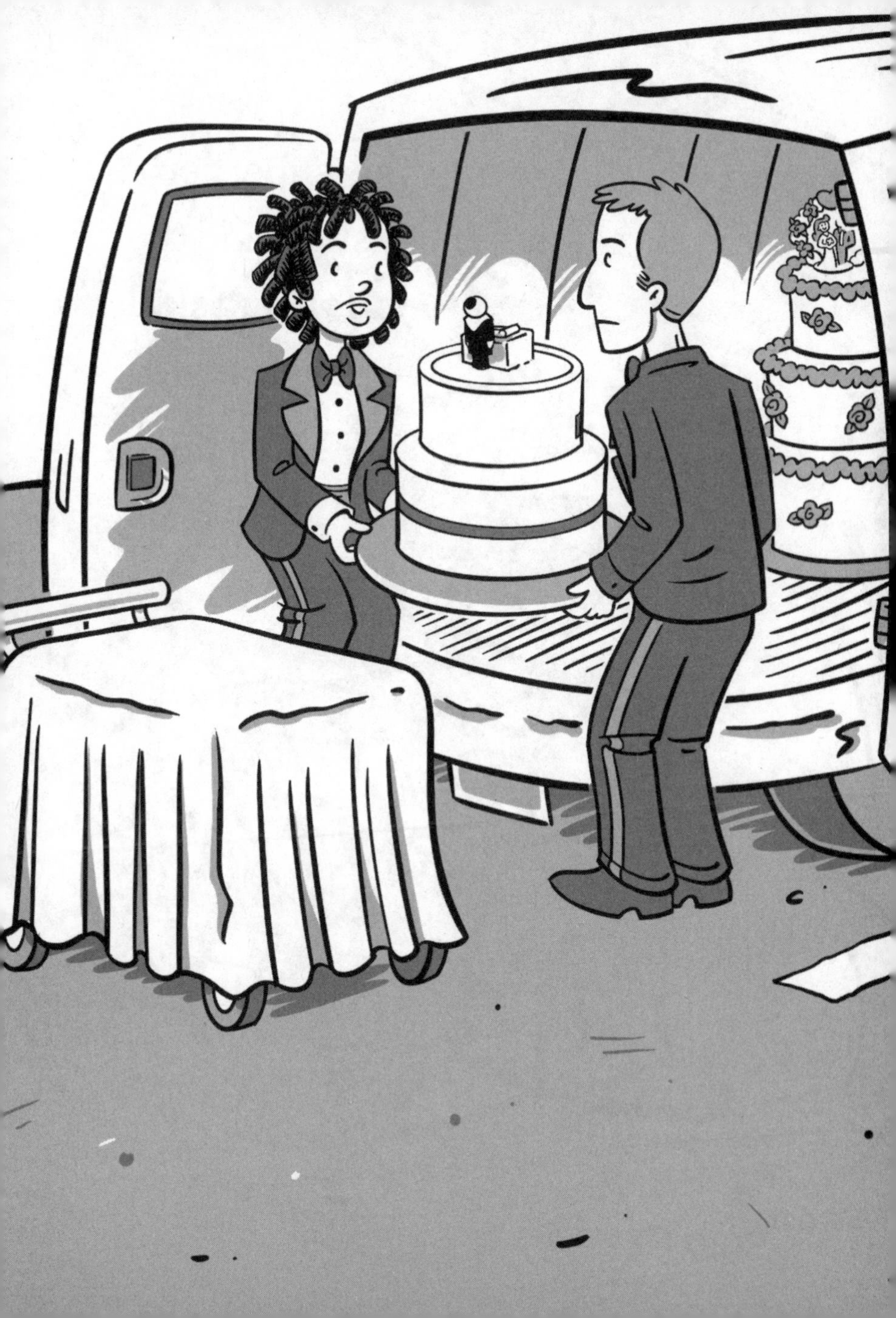

CHAPTER 9

Mazel Tov!

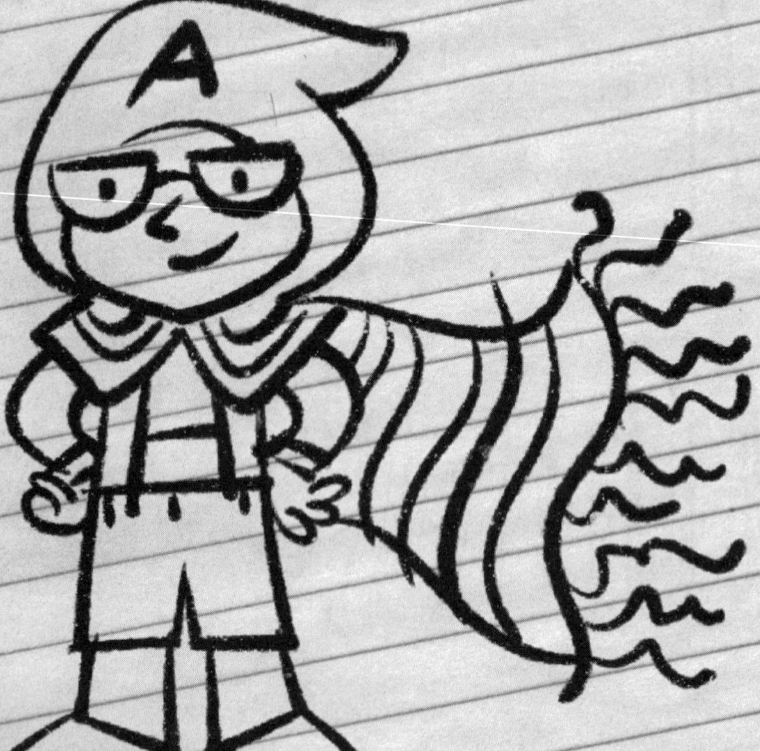

By
Eugene

Nacho Cheese Man whipped out a can of string cheese. "Take this cheese, evil spy-waiters!"

Strings of cheese blasted from the can and hit the two waiters.

"Hey! What are you doing?" the waitress shouted.

Captain Awesome leaped
forward and struck a cool superhero
pose. "We're stopping you from
stealing the wedding cake!"

"We know you're working for
Tiramisunami!" Supersonic Sal
cried out. "We're here to stop you!"

The two waiters looked confused. "Tiramisu-what? Is that another catering company?"

"If you're not working for the dessert diva of badness, then who's your evil leader?!" Captain Awesome asked.

"Um . . . the manager, I guess?" the waitress answered. "She can be grumpy sometimes, but I wouldn't call her evil."

"Where is she?" Nacho Cheese Man pulled out a can of spicy cheddar cheese. "Tell us!"

"The manager isn't here," the waiter replied.

"Then who's giving you orders?!" Supersonic Sal asked.

"The bride's parents," the waitress replied.

GASP! SHOCK! DOUBLE SHOCK!

"The bride's parents?! It's an inside job?!" Captain Awesome said.

Supersonic Sal was stunned. "If you're taking orders from my cousin's family, then why do you have ear walkie-talkies?!"

"Yeah! I bet you can't explain that!" Nacho Cheese Man added.

"Sure we can," the waitress answered. "This is how we talk with the other waiters. Whenever someone needs help, we just say it over the mics."

"Good service is priority number one!" the waiter said proudly.

"More like evil service," Captain Awesome corrected. "Why are the bride's parents trying to sabotage their daughter's wedding?"

All of a sudden, a realization hit Captain Awesome harder than Dr. Drumbledore's Weapons of Mass Percussion had hit Super Dude in the *Super Dude Musical Spectacular.* "They want you to steal the cake because they don't want any of us to have a slice?!"

Now the waiters looked even more confused.

"No one's trying to sabotage the wedding," the waitress said.

"This is the wrong cake!" the waiter said. "It was accidentally dropped off here, and we were going to switch it for the right cake so their special day wouldn't be ruined," the waitress explained.

Captain Awesome, Supersonic Sal, and Nacho Cheese Man took a closer look at the cake. Mazel tov, Nathan, on your bar mitzvah! was written on the cake in frosting.

"Who's Nathan?" Supersonic Sal asked.

"Dunno," Nacho Cheese Man said. "But if he's getting a whole cake, he's one lucky kid."

The pieces of the puzzle suddenly fell into place. "So you're *not* trying to steal the wedding cake?" Supersonic Sal asked. "You're trying to fix a cake mix-up?"

"Exactly!" The waitress opened the back of the van to reveal a second cake. White frosting! Three levels! With a tiny bride and groom on top!

"Wow! It's even cooler than Nathan's cake!" Captain Awesome said.

The waitress tried to pick up the wedding cake, but it was too big for one person. The top tier wobbled and almost fell.

"Look out!" Supersonic Sal jumped forward and steadied the cake.

"Getting this cake into the wedding's going to be harder than I thought," the concerned waitress said.

"Never fear, good citizen!" Captain Awesome called out as he and Nacho Cheese Man joined Supersonic Sal. "With the Sunnyview Superhero Squad's help, it'll be a piece of cake!"

CHAPTER 10

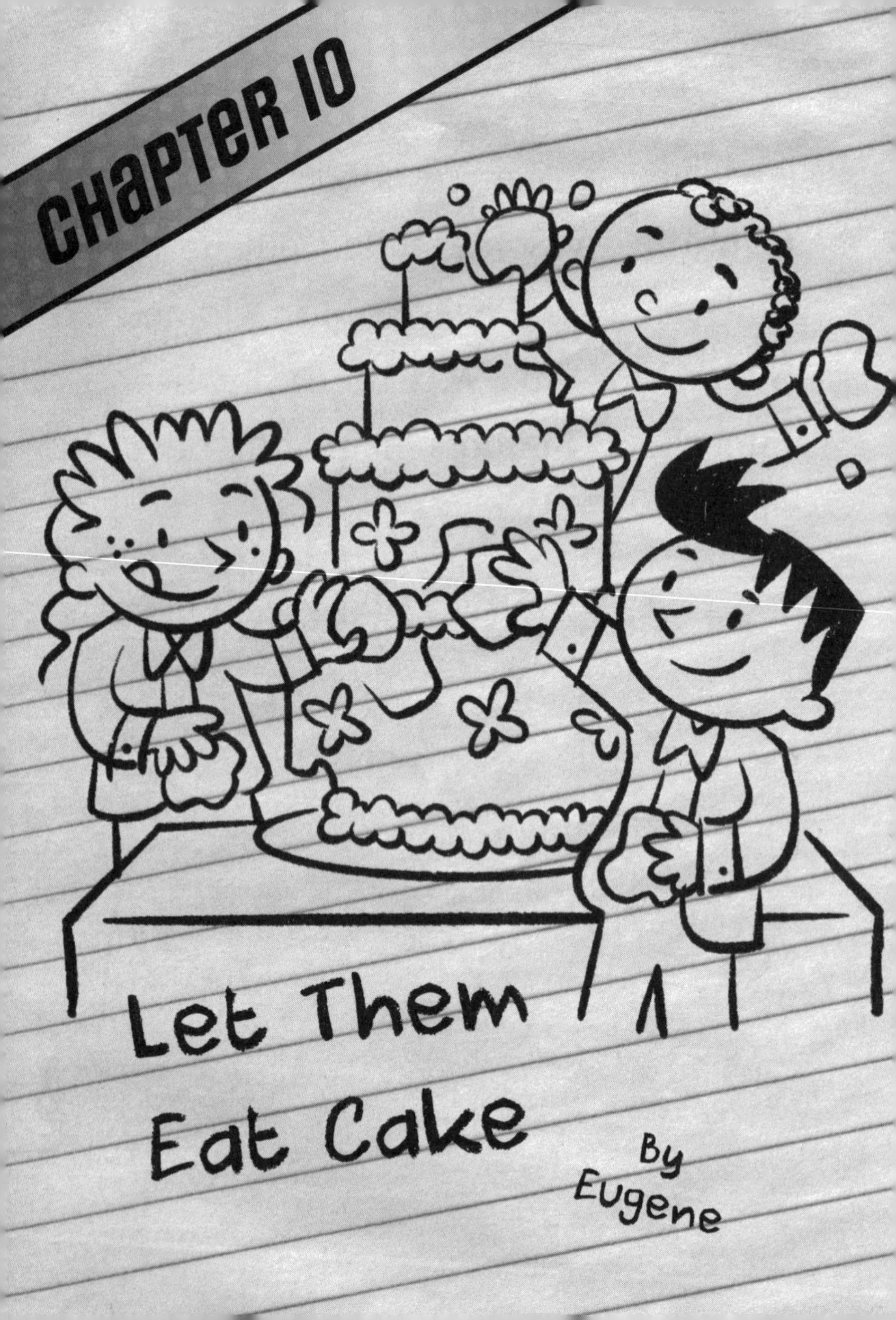

Let Them Eat Cake

By Eugene

"This . . . is . . . the . . . best . . . cake . . . EVER!" Eugene cheered, already on his third slice.

"Agreed," Charlie said, squirting some cheese frosting onto his slice.

Sally laughed. "And all it took to get a slice was almost getting our brains melted on the dance floor."

With the case solved and the wedding cake saved, the three kids had returned their superhero outfits to their backpacks and were enjoying the wedding cake together.

Even Eugene's sister, Molly, was enjoying a slice, which she mashed onto her face as she tried to eat it.

"There may not have been evil bad guys, but we still saved the day," Eugene said. "It's like Super Dude always says: 'You don't need to fight a supervillain to be a hero. You just need to help someone who needs it.'"

"And hopefully you'll get cake when you do!" Charlie added.

"Looks like you three are finally enjoying the wedding," Mrs. McGillicudy said as she and Eugene's dad joined them.

"I don't know if we're enjoying the *wedding*, exactly," Eugene replied. "But we sure are enjoying the wedding cake."

His parents laughed.

"Because you guys were such good sports, we got you a little surprise," Eugene's mom said.

Eugene's dad pulled out three copies of Super Dude's Ultra-Mega Edition.

"NO WAY!" Eugene, Charlie, and Sally gasped.

"It's the double-size Super Dude Ultra-Mega issue with Ultra Super Dude Super Stickers!" Eugene cheered.

"Cake, canned cheese, and Super Dude?! This really is the best wedding ever!" Charlie said.

"Do you think Super Dude has ever been to a wedding?" Sally asked.

"Don't you remember Super Dude number three hundred twenty-four?!" Eugene replied. "Super Dude had to stop the Bride of Prankenstein from replacing all the wedding gifts with yucky spinach!"

As Sally and Charlie read their
Super Dude comics and enjoyed
their cake, Eugene looked out over
the packed dance floor.

"We can read later!" Eugene
said to Sally and Charlie. "It's time
to boogie!"

Eugene grabbed Charlie's and Sally's hands, and the best friends raced out to join their families.

This wedding wasn't so bad after all, Eugene thought. *Even with all the pink and glitter everywhere.*

Actually, it was kind of . . .

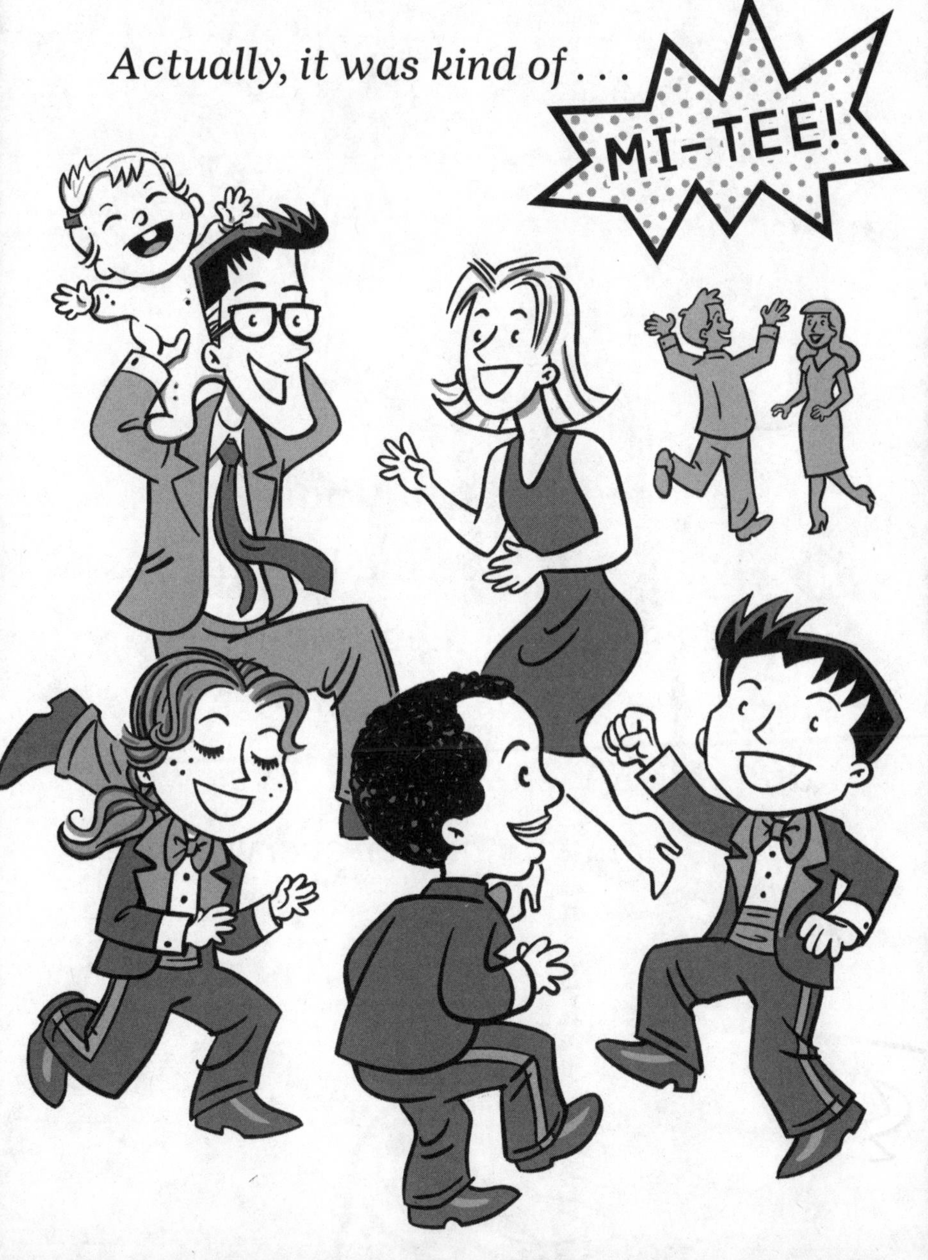
MI-TEE!

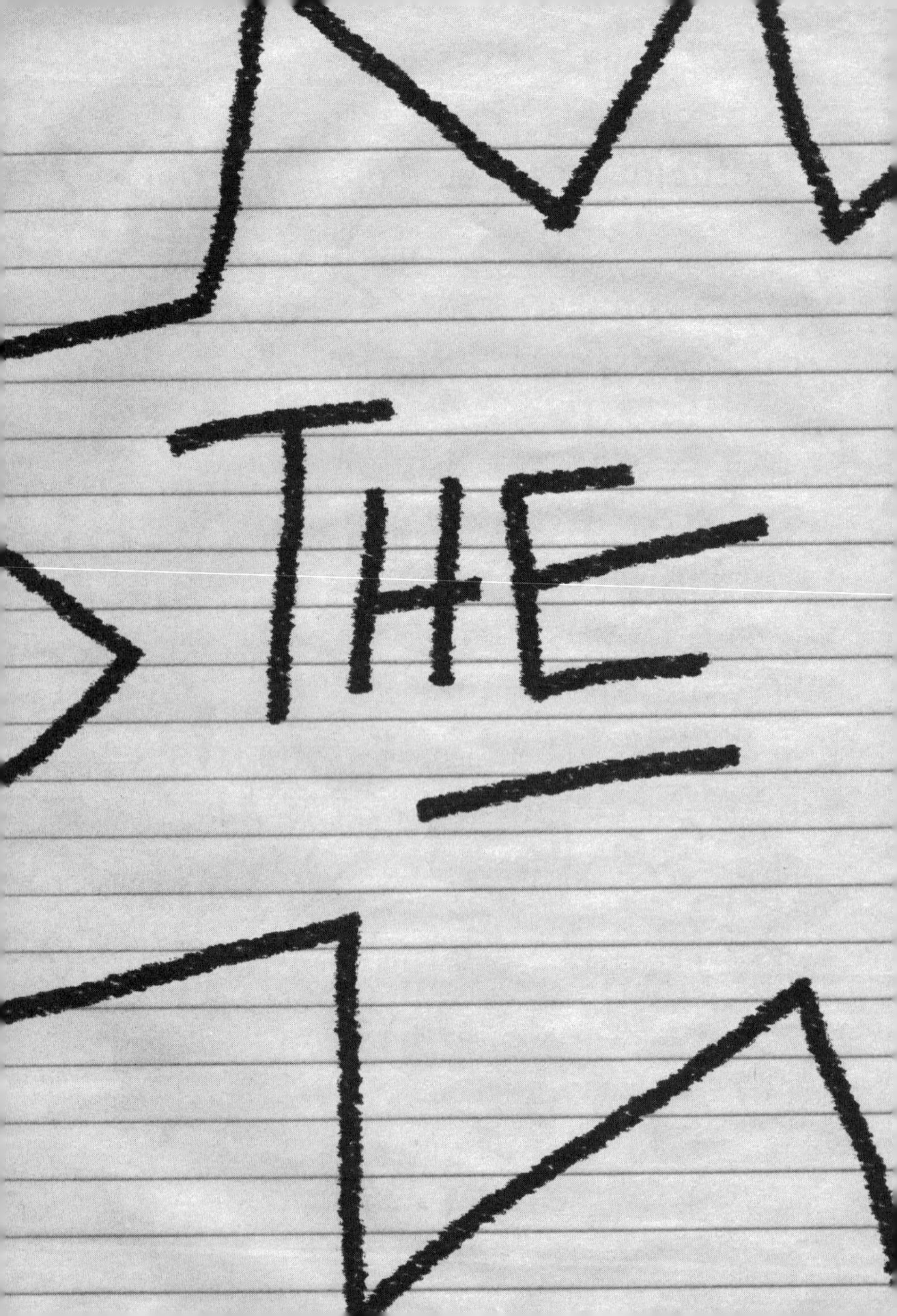
THE

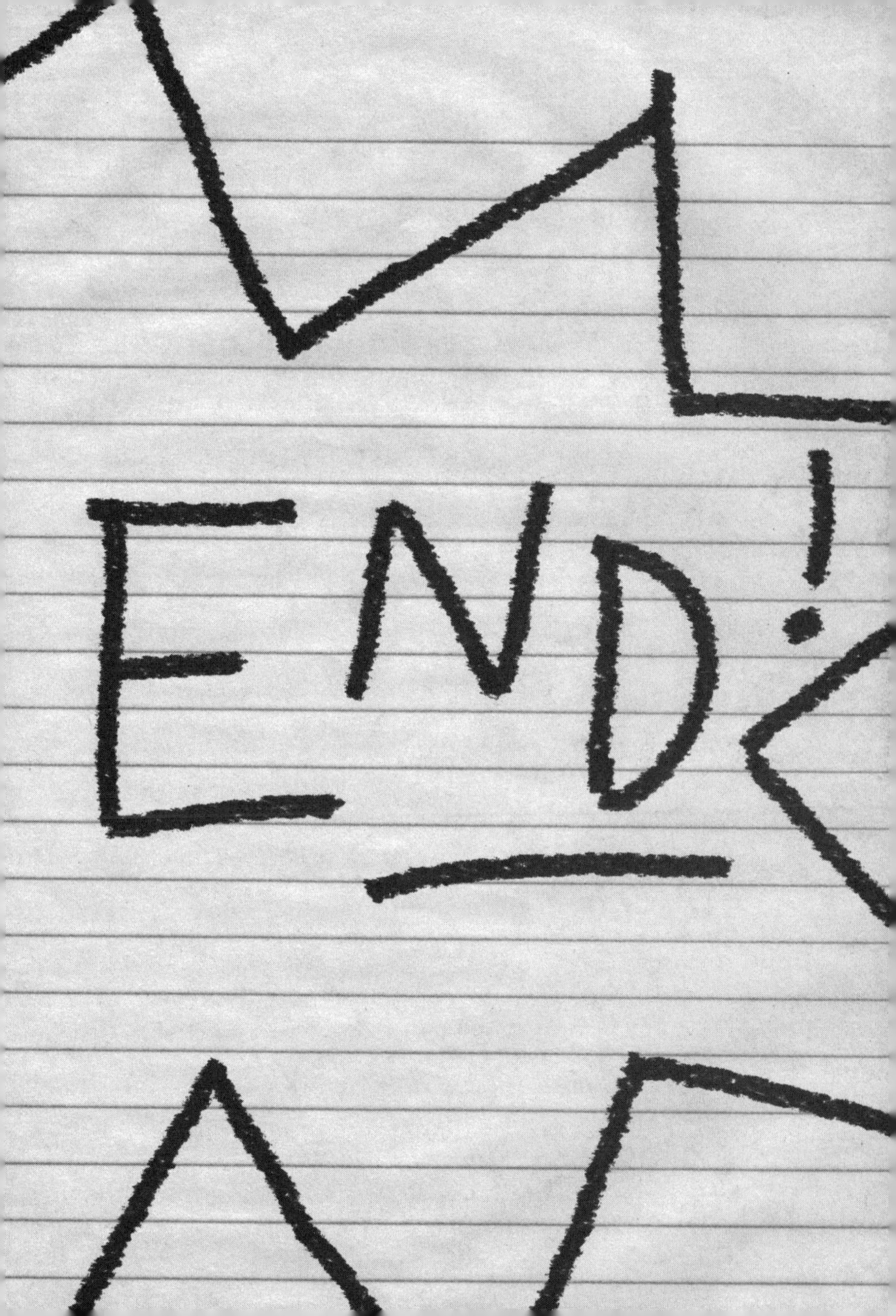

THE END!

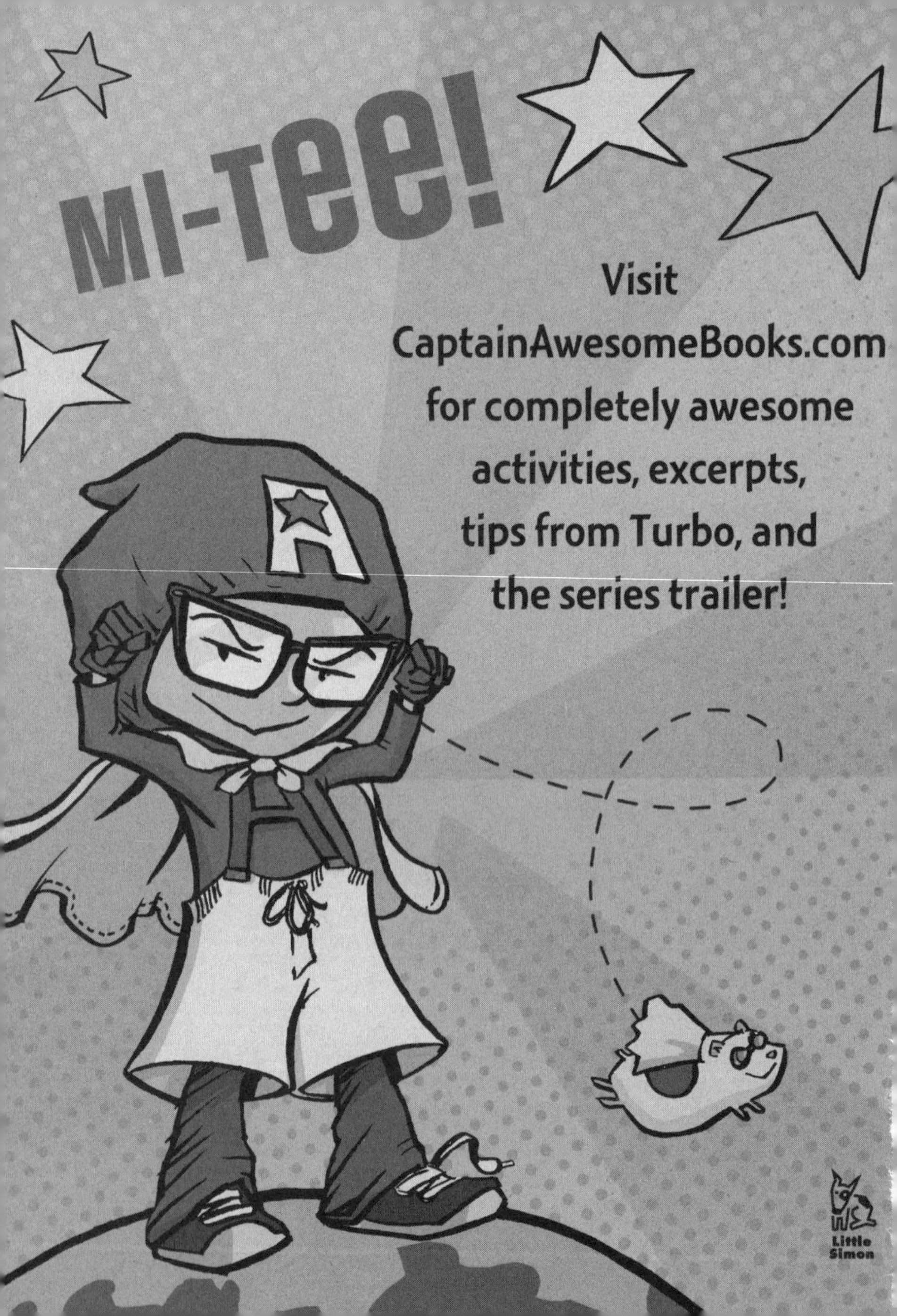
MI-TEE!
Visit
CaptainAwesomeBooks.com
for completely awesome
activities, excerpts,
tips from Turbo, and
the series trailer!
Little
Simon